A Giant First-Start Reader

This easy reader contains only 45 different words, repeated often to help the young reader develop word recognition and interest in reading.

Basic word list for *Three Little Chicks*

a	eggs	pops
all	for	she
alone	happy	soft
and	he	the
another	is	there
are	Jenny	three
Benny	little	time
but	now	together
calls	of	too
can	one	two
chick	open	what
chicks	out	who
crack	peep	will
cracking	Penny	with
egg	play	yellow

Three Little Chicks

Written by Kathy Feczko

Illustrated by Paul Harvey

Troll Associates

Library of Congress Cataloging in Publication Data

Feczko, Kathy.
    Three little chicks.

    Summary: Three little chicks hatch out of their eggs
and play together.
    1. Children's stories, American. [1. Chickens—
Fiction] I. Harvey, Paul, 1926-   ill. II. Title.
PZ7.F9298Th . 1985   [E]   84-8629
ISBN 0-8167-0355-8 (lib. bdg.)

10 9 8 7 6 5 4 3 2 1

Three little eggs.

One...two...three little eggs.

Crack…crack…crack!

One of the eggs is cracking open.

Out of the egg pops Benny!

Benny is a little chick.
He is soft and yellow.

"Peep, peep, peep!" calls Benny.

But Benny is all alone.

Crack...crack...crack!

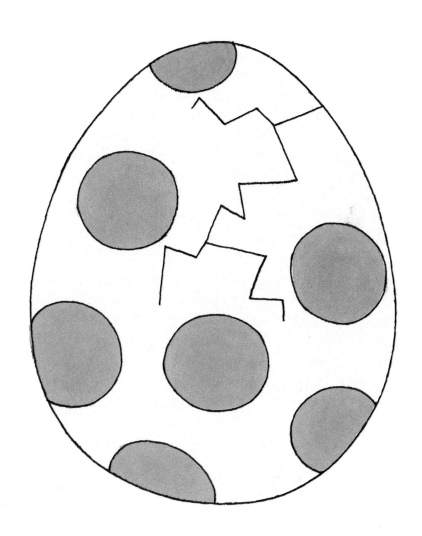

Another egg

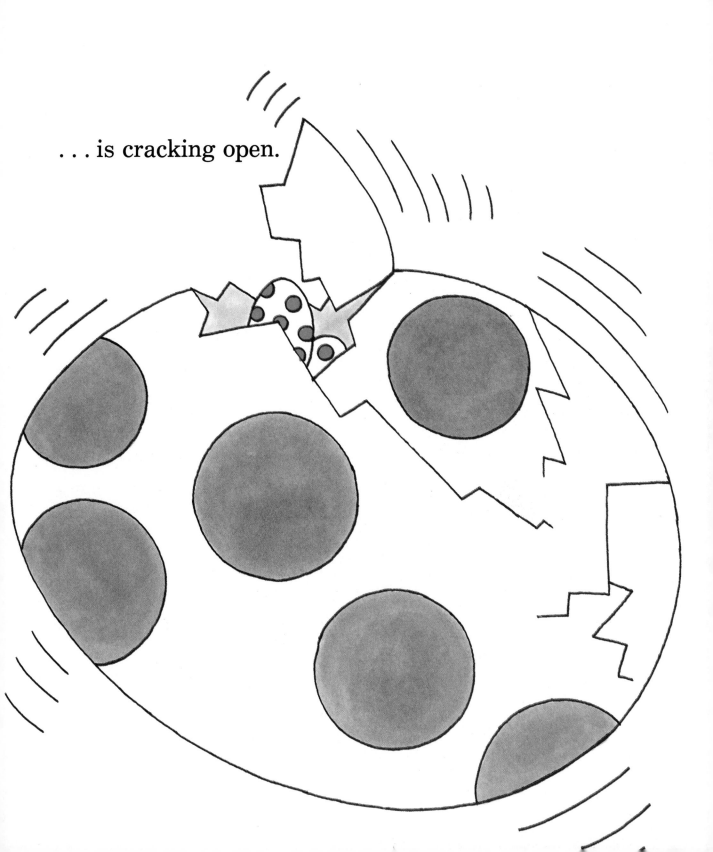

. . . is cracking open.

Out of the egg pops Jenny!

Jenny is a little chick, too.
She is soft and yellow.

"Peep, peep, peep!" calls Jenny.
Now there are two little chicks.

Jenny will play with Benny!

Crack…crack…crack!

Another egg is cracking open.

Out of the egg pops Penny.

Penny is a little chick, too.

She is soft and yellow.
"Peep, peep, peep!" calls Penny.

Now there are three little chicks.

Penny will play with Benny and Jenny.

The three little chicks can play together.

What a happy time for three little chicks!
Peep, peep, peep.